To every child who loves a special book

This paperback edition first published in 2015 by Andersen Press Ltd.
First published in Great Britain in 2015 by Andersen Press Ltd., 20 Vauxhall Bridge Road, London SW1V 2SA.
Published in Australia by Random House Australia Pty., Level 3, 100 Pacific Highway, North Sydney, NSW 2060.

Copyright © 2014 by Bob Staake.
Published by arrangement with Random House Children's Books,
a division of Random House LLC, New York, USA.
The rights of Bob Staake to be identified as the author and illustrator of this work have been asserted by him in
accordance with the Copyright, Designs and Patents Act, 1988.
All rights reserved. Printed and bound in Malaysia by Tien Wah Press.

10   8   6   4   2   1   3   5   7   9

British Library Cataloguing in Publication Data available.

ISBN 978 1 78344 231 7

MY PET BOOK

Bob Staake

Andersen Press

Most pets, you know, are cats and dogs.
Go out and take a look.
But there's a boy in Smartytown
whose pet's… a little book.

He never cared for puppy dogs,
and kittens made him sneezy.
He pleaded with his mum and dad,
"I want a pet that's easy!"

"A book would make the perfect pet!"
He heard his mother say.
And Dad had read that no pet book
had ever run away.

So they strolled right past the pet shop
to a place with books for sale.
Not one had whiskers, fur, or fleas,
or a waggy little tail!

How could the boy pick out just one?
Too tough for this book lover.
But then a small book caught his eye…

a frisky red hardcover!

Of all the books stocked in the shop,
he liked this one the best!
The pages crisp, the printing fine,
much redder than the rest.
He didn't need to give his pet
a name, like Rex or Sport.
It wouldn't answer anyway,
and so the book was bought!

It never ate. It never drank.
It couldn't do a trick.
It never shed. It had no fleas.
It couldn't fetch a stick.

It never needed bathing,
and its ears would never droop.
But best of all, that little pet...
it didn't even poop!

A better pet you couldn't have
for graceful evening strolls.
(It wasn't like those ill-bred dogs
that drink from toilet bowls,
or like a cat that always sleeps,
or won't turn off its purr.)
A pet book never makes a sound,
and doesn't lick its fur.

Inside the book were many tales
of bravery and glory.
The boy imagined as he read
that he was *in* the story!

The boy would leave his pet at home
when off to school he'd go.

But one day when
the boy returned,

the book
was gone…

"My book's run off! My book's run off!"
The boy began to bleat.
"How could my book run out on me
without a pair of feet?"

The maid could hear the crying boy
and came without delay.

"I think I know what happened…" *(gulp)*
"I gave your book…

away."

While cleaning junk out of the house,
the maid had grabbed a box
and filled it full of household things,
like cups and plates and socks.

She must have swept the book up too,
and simply sealed the top.
And then the maid took box and all
to the local charity shop!

They raced straight there hoping they
would find it on a shelf,
just sitting there and waiting
near a dusty Christmas elf.

It wasn't hanging with the coats,
or sitting with the chairs!
The pet book wasn't with the lamps,
or snoozing with stuffed bears!

Of course they went through all the books,
the new ones and the old.
The pet book wasn't anywhere.
It must have just been…

SOLD!

They slumped down on an old settee,
and cried and cried and cried.
But then the maid leaned in and asked…

"Where would a pet book hide?"

The boy had never thought of that.
He broke into a smile,
remembering something he had seen
in the dog-and-cat-stuff aisle.

"If I were just a scared pet book,
I'd likely sneak in here.
Perhaps the dark would help me hide,
and make me disappear!"

Then with his hand the boy reached in,
to feel around each nook.
And then he pulled it out because…

he'd found his lost pet book!

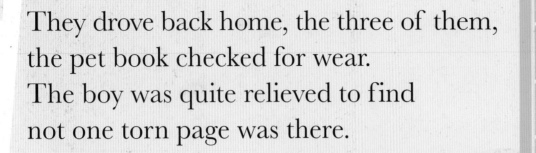

They drove back home, the three of them,
the pet book checked for wear.
The boy was quite relieved to find
not one torn page was there.

A crazy day they'd had indeed,
yet the story ended well.
And now the boy and his pet book
had their own tale to tell.

The boy's mum gently asked him
how a book could bring such joy.
"Because every book's a *friend*!"
explained the yawning little boy.

His eyes were sleepy from the search
and all the time it took.
But now the boy could dream
all night…

with his lost – and found – pet book.